NEVER SAY NEVER

PALMETTO
P U B L I S H I N G
Charleston, SC
www.PalmettoPublishing.com

Copyright © 2023 by Tony L. Smith

All rights reserved

No portion of this book may be reproduced, stored in a retrieval system, or transmitted in any form by any means–electronic, mechanical, photocopy, recording, or other–except for brief quotations in printed reviews, without prior permission of the author.

Paperback ISBN: 979-8-8229-2882-4

Never Say Never

TONY L. SMITH

CHAPTER 1

I could feel something special happening that day. It was a very hot day in July. I was driving to Costco to get my sister a cake for her birthday on Sunday. That's when I looked over in the next lane and saw the most beautiful woman God had ever put on this earth. We were driving side by side. When she looked over at me and smiled, I returned the smile and pointed at my ring finger—it was a gesture asking her if she was married. Still smiling, she shook her head no. She then motioned for me to pull over on the expressway in the emergency lane. I pulled up behind her and sat in my Lincoln Navigator while she got out of her car. She walked toward my truck as I stared at her. She had the most beautiful caramel skin, and her hair was cut short in a Halle Berry–type style. It had fallen because her car didn't have air.

The air-conditioning in her car was broken, but that didn't stop her from looking like an angel that was lost and trying to find her way back to heaven. She was about 5'1" with a body to kill for. Her skin was smooth and bronze—she was a perfect ten. When she walked up to my driver's side door, I rolled my window down, smiled, and said, "Hi." She smiled again. This time my heart raced at a frantic pace. Her eyes were very beautiful and captivating. They were emerald green, and they glared in the sun. Her lips were full and hypnotizing as I watched them and licked my own dry lips.

"Hi, I'm Nikki Adams."

I was so intrigued by her beauty I almost didn't hear her. Making my best attempt to speak without getting tongue tied and making a fool of myself, I said, "I'm Rome, Romeo Daniels."

"Well, Mr. Daniels, is this your regular routine, riding on the freeway flirting with women?"

I laughed and said, "No, I only do this twice a week," and Nikki laughed. She was sweating from being in a hot car and now from standing in the sun. I looked her over. She was wearing a uniform—Nikki was a deputy sheriff. I then asked her if she had a number that I could reach her at later. She took my phone out of my hand, typed in her number, and gave it back to me. She then said she was headed home to take a shower and lie under the air. I told her she'd better hurry before she melted; we both laughed as she said bye, got in her car, and drove off. I then continued my journey to Costco.

In Costco I walked toward the bakery area. When I arrived, I searched for the perfect cake for my big sis. When I found it, I stood in line to order it. There were about six people in front of me. I waited patiently. After a while my mind started wandering. Was this what I really wanted? Another relationship? Nikki was a goddess, but the pain a woman could cause was like no other. I had experienced it firsthand.

I started thinking about the event that had happened two weeks ago when my ex-wife and I got into a heated spat. I had moved into my new place a few days before our divorce was finalized. I went to the house we once shared to get my remaining items. Keisha (my ex-wife) and her mother were sitting in the living room. I walked in and didn't say a word. I walked down the hallway to the bedroom to get my things, with Keisha following close behind. When I tried to open the closet door, it wouldn't open. I looked down, and there were two duffel bags on the floor blocking the door. One was slightly unzipped. I could see that there were men's clothes in the bag, and they weren't mine. No doubt they belonged to the guy I'd found out Keisha was cheating with. I picked up the bags, never saying a word, and threw them. Clothes flew everywhere. I opened the closet door and got my bags, and before I walked out of the room, I turned to Keisha and asked, "Does his wife know that he's over here?" Keisha looked at me with a smirk on her face and said to me, "Don't you worry about that." Then she coldly said, "I'm his wife." I lost it! With my bags in my left hand, I smacked Keisha with my right. She flew from one side of the room into the wall on the other side. I found out firsthand that temporary insanity was real, because I didn't remember what happened after that. I can only say that when I came to my senses, I was standing on the front porch with my bags in my hand. Keisha's mother was standing in the door yelling at me, with a knife in her hand, telling me to leave before she called the police. I left and didn't look back. So now I was back at this point, not sure if I ever wanted a serious relationship again.

"May I help you?" the lady behind the counter asked. I proceeded to tell her which cake I wanted and told her I would pick it up on Sunday. I then returned home. When I walked in, I placed my keys on the table. I then sat on my sofa and pressed play on my answering machine. The first message was from my sister Pam telling me she had cooked and if I was hungry to come by. I was hungry, but I was too tired to eat. In reality I didn't want to make the drive. Pam was more of a mother figure than a sister. Mainly because we were the only two children and our parents were killed in a car crash nine years ago. Pam was older than me—she was thirty-four, about to turn thirty-five in a couple of days. I was twenty-eight, but the way Pam looked after me, you would think that I was eight. The second message was from Thomas Miller, aka "Tank," my best friend and co-owner of the law firm Daniels and Miller, which was located in the downtown area of Memphis, Tennessee. He wanted me to go to the Heavenly Hideout with him. It was a new strip club that had just opened up. I said to myself, I will call him back later. It was a little after 5:00 p.m., so I decided to lie down on the sofa to watch *SportsCenter*. After a few minutes, *SportsCenter* was watching me. I woke up and looked over at the clock. It was 8:30 p.m.

I called Tank and told him to roll through about ten o'clock. Tank said cool, he'd be over. I got up, went upstairs to my bedroom closet, and took out the linen set that I had gotten out to the cleaners yesterday. I placed it neatly on my bed. I took my clothes off and turned on the water in my shower, and before I got in, I glanced over at my body-length mirror and saw a black Adonis. I was 6'3" and 225 pounds, rock solid. I was never the type of guy to be stuck on myself, but it was more that I loved myself as a person and I was comfortable in my own skin. Even through it all, to myself I still had imperfections. I stepped into the shower and thought about what it would have been like if Nikki were in the shower with me. I started rubbing my arms, chest, shoulders, and thighs. Lost in a daze of fantasizing, I started to stroke myself, thinking of how good it would feel to have Nikki's beautiful lips on mine and then all over my body. The more I thought, the more intense the pleasure became. All of a sudden, like a swift wind, I came. The pressure was so intense I had to grab the shower bar to keep from hitting the floor, from nearly passing out. I quickly lathered up really good, washed off, and jumped out of the shower. I looked at the clock, and time had started to pass, so I dried off quickly, got dressed, and put on my Acqua Di Gio cologne.

At that time my doorbell was ringing. By the continuous, nonstop ringing, I knew it was Tank. When I opened the door, like his normal self, loud and obnoxious, Tank yelled, "Damn, you gonna let a brother in or what?" I then greeted him with our brotherly handshake and hug. "So you ready to roll or what?" Tank asked.

"Ready?" I replied. "Man, you drive so slow I was about to get ready for bed." We both laughed.

Tank said "Let's go do the damn thang" as we walked out to his car. We were on our way to the Heavenly Hideout. The night was calm and a little cooler than earlier in the day when the sun was out, but not by much. I started telling Tank about the event earlier in the day, when I met Nikki and got her phone number. He asked me why I took her number and said I might as well hand it over to him because I was never gonna use it. I thought maybe Tank was right—after all the bull I went through with Keisha, I knew I was never gonna give a woman my heart again. I finally came to my senses and said hell no. I was taking advice from Tank? He was the most dog-ass brother a woman could meet. If Tank met a woman and they didn't have sex the same night, she never heard from him again. I told him yeah, I was gonna use Nikki's number. Now don't get me wrong, he can give you some hellified legal advice, but advice on relationships, if Tank ever gave you advice on it, you'd better do the opposite of whatever he said or you would be saying goodbye to that relationship.

We arrived at the club. Tank got valet service. We walked through the first set of doors, strolling along a red carpet. We stopped at the window as we paid to get in. Tank then gave the man behind the glass a big head hundred and asked for a hundred ones. We then followed the red carpet to a second set of doors. As we walked through, there was this fine-ass, butt-naked babe standing there. She was out of view from the first entrance. She patted me down to make sure I didn't have any weapons and told me to go on in and have a good time. Tank was next, and with him I knew something was bound to happen. She patted Tank down, then grabbed his dick and told him to go on in and have a good time. Right on cue Tank didn't disappoint: his freaky ass grabbed the lady by her titties and smacked her on the ass and said he was already having a great time.

We went on in the club and found some nice seats close to the stage. The set was very elegant and classy. The waitress came over took our drink order; then she disappeared, headed toward the bar area. I then focused on my surroundings and noticed that there were titties and ass everywhere. This is one of the rare occasions Tank's talking ass is quiet—when he's focused on some ass. However, that's my dog. We were really digging the scenery, the music, and especially the hugs and squeezes from the women. The attention was nice all of a sudden. Every woman I saw in the club started looking like Nikki. At this point I'm thinking to myself, I know I'm not fucked up that quick—I mean, I only have had three drinks. I look again, and I'm still seeing Nikki's face, that beautiful smile and those beautiful eyes. By now I'm thinking, Who the fuck put something in my drink? Reality settled in, and I realized that Nikki's beauty had taken over my thoughts several times today. I would never tell Tank what I had just experienced. He would probably say that I was bugging out. I looked over at Tank, and he was headed to the VIP area with three women. I slyly grinned and thought, Selfish muthafucka. I turned my focus back to the stage and finished enjoying the show. A little later I took a dancer up on her offer: a dance in the VIP area, or as Chris Rock might say, the champagne room. It was about two in the morning, so we decided to head out. Tank didn't get any numbers, so I guessed after he dropped me off he was heading home. I got out and told Tank I'd holler at him later. I went in the house, got undressed, got in my bed, and went to sleep.

CHAPTER 2

It was early Saturday morning when my phone rang. I reached over and knocked the phone to the floor trying to answer it. I was so tired I almost fell out of bed trying to get it. I answered the phone with a very sleepy hello. "Wake up, sleepyhead," the voice on the other end said. It was Pam. "Why haven't you called, and where have you been?" she asked.

"I worked a little late on a hectic case. After that I had a little running around to do after I left the office," I said. Pam wanted to know if I could help Chuck put up a few picnic tables and help him cut the yard in preparation for her birthday dinner tomorrow. Chuck was Pam's husband. As usual I couldn't turn Pam down.

"Ok, I'll be over later," I said. I then told Pam that I might be bringing a friend to her birthday dinner.

"That's fine," Pam said. Then she asked, "Wait, it's not Keisha, is it?" I could hear the sarcasm in her voice.

"Hell no!" I replied. "I wouldn't take that bitch to a dogfight."

Pam started laughing. She had never liked Keisha from the very first time they met. It was mainly because of Keisha's I'm-all-that-ass attitude—everybody was beneath her.

"I met someone, and I wanted to invite her to your dinner," I said.

Pam told me that was cool with her. Pam then asked, "Is the damn fool Tank gonna come?"

"He wouldn't miss it for the world. As long as women are gonna be there, Tank is gonna be there."

Pam and I both laughed. I then told her I would be by later. I got up, took a shower, put on my khaki shorts and a wifebeater, went downstairs, and fixed me a bowl of cereal. I sat at the kitchen table and read the morning paper. When I finished that, I cleaned and dusted my house. I went into my office and placed files that I would be working on Monday on top of my desk so I would remember to take them to the firm. When I finished I went into the den, sat on my sofa, and pressed the button for my TV. While I waited for the screen to lower itself from the ceiling, I picked up the phone and Nikki's number, which I had placed on the end of the table. I dialed the number. After three rings I was about to hang up, and Nikki answered it. "Hello," her lovely voice said.

I got chills, and a lump formed in my throat. I cleared my throat and asked, "Hey, beautiful, are you busy?"

I could sense a smile on Nikki's face as she said, "Oh, not on the expressway today?"

As she had said it jokingly, I laughed and said, "No, it's too early."

Nikki told me no, she wasn't busy. As a matter of fact, she was just coming in from a morning jog—got to keep the heart healthy and the body tight.

"No doubt," I replied. "I am calling to see if you would like to go with me to my sister's birthday dinner tomorrow evening if you aren't busy."

"I'm free after church. I'd love to go."

"All right, then it's a date," I replied.

"Our first date," Nikki said.

"Well, actually, I wanted to know if I could take you out to dinner or a late lunch. If you aren't busy," I said.

Nikki said, "Well, I have to take my mother to the grocery store and to the mall a little later. After that we can go out."

"Ok, take my number and give me a call when you get in."

"That's fine," Nikki said.

"Ok, I'll talk to you later then," I said.

Nikki told me bye, and we hung up. I then sat back on my couch. The TV was on, but I wasn't paying it any attention. Instead I was thinking how nice it was to talk on the phone to a female voice other than Pam. But I promised myself I wasn't going past friendship, no matter how fine Nikki was, because I said a woman would never have my heart again. With that said, I jumped up, grabbed my keys off the table, and headed to Pam's house.

When I arrived at Pam's, she greeted me at the door with a giant hug and kiss on my cheek. "What up, what up?" I said.

"Nothing much. Just working like a slave trying to get everything together," Pam said.

"Where's Chuck?" I asked.

"He's gone to Walmart to get some charcoal for tomorrow and some dog food for Judo." Chuck busted his ass to make sure Pam was happy. There wasn't shit he wouldn't do for her, and vice versa. I was just happy to know she didn't dog Chuck out like a lot of women do to nice guys. She treated him like a king, and he treated her like the black queen that she is. On the issue of treating nice guys wrong, it works the other way as well, and Tank is living proof. Thank God he and I are the exact opposite of each other. Maybe that's why we get along so well.

"Big sis, where's the lawn mower?" I asked.

"It's out back in the storage house," Pam said. I went out, got it, and went to work. Later Pam brought me a tall glass of lemonade and a towel to wipe my head and face.

When I got ready to start back cutting the grass, I heard someone yell, "Yo, Rome, what's up?" I turned around, and it was my brother-in-law, Chuck. We gave each other dap and the brotherly hug. "I see Pam's got you sweating like a hog," Chuck said and laughed.

"Man, yeah, I probably couldn't have gotten out of cutting this weekend if I'd wanted to," I said.

"Well, carry on, my friend," Chuck said. I started the mower back up and started cutting the yard. Chuck got the edger, and he edged the yard. And then he shaped up the flower bed. When we finished the yard, it looked like it had been done by landscape professionals. We went in the house. Pam was washing dishes. She had fixed Chuck a plate and asked me if I wanted a plate. I told her no thanks—I was going out to dinner with Nikki.

"Uh-huh, Nikki," Pam said. "Is it serious?" Pam asked.

Before I could answer Pam, Chuck laughed and said, "Aha, getting your feet wet again?"

To answer Pam I said, "No!" And as for Chuck, I told him, "This heart is under lock and key. Never again." And with that I kissed Pam on her cheek, patted Chuck on his back, and told them I would see them later. They both said bye.

I went home and turned on my answering machine. Nikki had left a message letting me know that she was home and I could call her when I got in. I first called Tank to let him know that Pam's dinner was gonna kick off around 6:00 p.m. Tank wasn't home, so I left the message on his answering machine.

Then I called Nikki. She answered on the second ring. "Hello," she said.

"Hello to you," I replied. "How did your day go?" I asked.

"Fine—I just thought my mother was gonna walk me to death. And how did yours go, Rome?" Nikki asked.

"I thought my sister was gonna work me to death." We both laughed. "So tell me—what are you in the mood for eating, Mrs. Physically Fit?"

Nikki laughed and said she loved seafood. Then she asked what about me. I told her, "Baby, you are talking to the seafood king." I told Nikki I love lobster, crab legs, crawfish, catfish, and skrimps. Nikki burst out in laughter. I didn't add my favorite seafood to the list: pussy. I kept that one in my head. I asked Nikki if she had a favorite seafood spot, and she said Red Lobster. "Perfect," I replied.

Nikki then said, "It's a date."

I told her that I was gonna go ahead take a shower and change. "So what if I pick you up at seven?" I asked.

"Seven is great," said Nikki.

"Ok, I will call you from my cell phone to get directions when I'm on my way." I told Nikki I would talk to her later. She said ok and bye.

With a little over an hour and a half to go, I quickly ran upstairs and took out my khakis and my black cotton Kenneth Cole button-up shirt, the one that fit me like a glove and showed off my muscular frame. I laid them on the bed and jumped in the shower. I showered in my Axe body wash, got out, and dried off and got dressed. I put on my Issey Miyake blue cologne and grabbed my keys and cell phone, and I was out of there.

I called Nikki as I pulled out of my driveway. She answered and gave me directions to her house. I knew exactly where she lived, on the east side of Memphis. I made a quick stop at the flower shop and got Nikki some roses. "Before you get carried away, I didn't say I wasn't a gentleman." I arrived at Nikki's house a little before seven. I rang the doorbell, and Nikki answered it. She opened the door, and I was greeted by that beautiful smile. Nikki looked stunning in her elegant black minidress by Vera Wang. She wore sexy heels that matched her dress, and her diamond necklace complemented her wardrobe. I looked at Nikki's beautiful face, and if you could imagine Sanaa Lathan mixed with Nia Long, you would come up with Nikki. I had my hand with the roses behind my back. Nikki looked me from head to toe and then softly bit her bottom lip, as if to say "Nice." I was hoping that after looking me over Nikki didn't see the hard-on she had given me. I swiftly brought my arm out from behind my back so Nikki could see the roses. Nikki placed both hands up to her mouth, and her captivating green eyes bulged with excitement and surprise. Nikki told me thank you, reached for the roses, then gave me a big hug. A little embarrassed, I knew she felt how hard and excited she had made me.

Nikki then told me to come in and have a seat while she put the roses in water. I sat on her comfortable plush sofa and told her she had a beautiful home. Nikki said thank you as she walked back into the living room. Nikki placed her vase of roses on her table; she got her purse and asked if I was ready. "Yes, Madame," I said in my best French voice. Nikki chuckled. We walked out, Nikki locked her door, and we walked to my truck. I opened Nikki's door, held her hand, and helped her in. I then got in on my side. I started my truck, and we were headed to Red Lobster.

On the way we talked a lot. I talked about my family, the firm, and the fact that I was newly divorced. I learned more about Nikki, her family, her job, and a couple of her relationships that didn't work out. In the beginning, I had wondered how such a beautiful woman could be all alone—now my questions were answered. Nikki told me that she was twenty-seven years old and her birthday was in September, the same month as mine.

We made it to Red Lobster. I got out, went around to Nikki's side, opened her door, and helped her out.

Her minidress was just above her tantalizing thighs. I was trying not to stare and give her the wrong impression. As we walked into the restaurant, Nikki locked her arm onto my arm. I felt really good. This let me know that she was comfortable. The hostess guided us to our seats. I pulled Nikki's chair back from the table so she could sit down; then I sat in my chair. The waitress soon came, and we placed our order. We started to converse again. I told Nikki that she was very beautiful and her dress was amazing. Nikki blushed and told me I was very handsome. I told her thanks. I then began to tell Nikki about a few of the people who were gonna be at Pam's dinner tomorrow. She laughed as I told her about Pam, Chuck, and a few other people that were close to Pam. I thought Nikki was gonna fall out of her chair when I gave her the scoop on Tank. Our food arrived and we began to eat. The conversations were great, and we had a lot of fun on our first date.

Nikki surprised me when she fed me one of her shrimps. Then I fed her a piece of my lobster tail. I dipped it in butter and placed it up to her mouth with my fork. Nikki opened her mouth, and the butter dripped on her lip as she ate the lobster. I wanted so bad to kiss the butter from Nikki's luscious lips. I remained cool and scooted back in my chair as we drank our apple martinis. I wanted Nikki to know I was having a great time. I reached over and gave her hand a gentle squeeze. Nikki was so relaxed she had taken her shoes off under the table. Before we realized it, we had spent well over three hours chatting, laughing, and having fun. We both knew it was getting late, and when we left, I took Nikki home. I walked her to the door and told her how much fun she was and that I had enjoyed the evening. Nikki said she had really enjoyed herself and told me thank you. I told her she was more than welcome. We hugged good night, and I drove home.

CHAPTER 3

I made it in, took off my clothes, put on my basketball shorts and a T-shirt, got in the bed, and crashed. As my body went deeper into sleep, I started to dream. I was lying on my back with no shirt on. That's when Nikki walked into my room. I was lying on my back staring at her in disbelief. With no words spoken between us, Nikki climbed on top of me, straddled me, and kissed my head, nose, and hungrily my lips. I returned the favor as we lay there passionately kissing. Nikki then slowly slid down my body, kissing every inch of me, making sure she didn't miss a spot. Nikki planted sweet little kisses on both sides of my neck and my ears, then moved down to both shoulders, to the center of my chest, to my right nipple and then my left as she gently bit me. I thought I was going to explode. Nikki made her way down to my stomach; then she started rubbing my thighs, then my balls and my dick. Nikki sighed with anticipation as she raised up and slid my boxers down and off. She let them hit the floor.

Then Nikki returned to where she had stopped. Nikki teased me by slowly licking the head of my dick and then the shaft. At this time, I was breathing very heavy from the pleasure Nikki was giving me. Nikki softly kissed and licked my balls, then came up and devoured my member into her hot and wanting mouth. What was moments of pleasure seemed like hours. After I couldn't take Nikki pleasing me any longer, I raised Nikki up to her feet and kissed her deeply. As I kissed her, I carefully removed Nikki's dress, and it accompanied my boxers on the floor. Nikki didn't have any garments on under her dress. I lowered my head to her breast, stuck out my tongue, and licked Nikki's hardened nipples. She threw her head back with her eyes closed, and a moan of pleasure escaped Nikki's lips. We stood there embracing as one. The heat from our bodies was so hot it felt like the room was on fire. I then laid Nikki down on the bed ever so gently and kissed her lips, breasts, stomach, thighs, and feet. I then licked and sucked each one of Nikki's toes with precision and care. Nikki's body shuddered in ecstasy.

I then raised up and went to the spot on her body I had intentionally missed. I was saving the best for last. As I placed my face in Nikki's pleasure garden, I took my time to savor the flavor of Nikki's area that was soaked and throbbing. I licked Nikki's clit entirely. I then licked and kissed her pussy lips, then went back to her pearl. I covered Nikki's flower opening with my tongue, making sure not to miss a drop or let any of her honey escape my mouth.

Nikki cried out as her body shook violently. She grabbed my bald head with both her hands. Nikki came hard, and I didn't stop. I wanted to please Nikki to the fullest. Nikki suddenly came again and again. Nikki's body begged me to fuck her, and I was more than a willing participant. I raised up from my lovely buffet. Nikki was still lying on her back, legs spread wide apart. I got on top of Nikki, but before I could penetrate her, Nikki grabbed my dick and shoved it inside her. Nikki yelled in ecstasy and pleasure as I pumped her long and hard. Nikki felt so good that I knew it wasn't gonna last much longer, so I went even faster and deeper. This time we were gonna enjoy this pleasurable sensation together. We both let out loud animal-sounding yells as we came together. Hoping the neighbors hadn't heard us and called the police, we both lay on the bed, spent. Nikki turned over, laid her head on my chest, and told me she loved me; I rubbed Nikki's back and said "I love you too."

Frantically I jumped and sat straight up in my bed, eyes widened like I was staring down the barrel of a loaded gun. My heart was racing faster than a wild pit bull. Finally I realized it was only a dream—better yet, a nightmare. I got up, face soaked from sweat, and went into the bathroom and washed it. I dried my face and threw the towel over in the hamper. I looked down and saw that I had the hardest erection I'd ever had in my life. I went over to the toilet and took a piss to release some pressure. I then went downstairs, got some water, and went back to bed.

It was finally morning; I got up and did a lot of running around. I was in and out of the house throughout the day. Time had passed, and it was almost time for Pam's birthday dinner. I call Nikki and told her after I got dressed I would come by and pick her up.

When I made it to Nikki's house, I was graced by her beauty before I could ring her doorbell. I looked at Nikki and said, "Nice."

Nikki then looked, smiled, and said, "You ain't bad either." We laughed. I gave her a hug. I thought to myself, Damn, she's fine. Nikki again didn't disappoint, looking lovely as ever. Nikki was wearing a sleeveless Ecko Red T-shirt, denim Ecko capris, and her all-white low-top Nike tennis shoes and Nike ankle socks. I wore my baby-blue Air Jordan T-shirt, Rocawear jean shorts, and my baby-blue-and-white Jordan tennis shoes. We then left Nikki's house and headed to Pam's.

When we arrived, we got out and noticed there were a lot of cars, certainly more than I'd expected. We went through the side gate that led into the back yard. When we made it into the back, there was a massive crowd. There were way more people here than I'd thought were gonna attend. Pam's birthday dinner turned out to be a birthday barbecue. People were dancing and playing cards and dominoes. I was greeted with half hugs and pats on my back. I couldn't shake hands because I was carrying Pam's birthday cake. It was so big I was trying to find a place to put it down. Nikki stayed very close, like she was scared she would lose me in the crowd. I placed the cake down on the picnic table where Pam was seated. Pam jumped up and shouted "Hey, handsome" as she walked toward me. We embraced each other. I kissed Pam on her jaw and told her happy birthday. Pam held her hand up toward my face. She smiled as she said, "Look what my husband got me—a two-carat diamond ring."

Jokingly, I asked Pam for her sunglasses to look at it, as if it were blinding me. The people around us started laughing. I then took out a gift I had gotten Pam. It was a diamond bracelet. Pam grabbed me again to give me a hug. "Thank you!" she screamed.

I finally got a chance to introduce Nikki to Pam. "Very pleased to meet you," Nikki said. Pam was still very excited about her diamond collection. Nikki laughed as Pam gave her a big hug.

"Where's my brother-in-law?" I asked Pam.

"He's over on the grill," she said. It was so crowded I hadn't seen him when we made it. Pam told me she had Nikki and was gonna show her around. Nikki smiled and told me to go ahead.

I walked over to Chuck and said, "What's up?" I told him I'd just seen his life's savings on my sister's finger, and we both laughed.

I felt someone touch me on my shoulder. I turned around, and it was Rochelle, Pam's friend, best friend to be exact. "Oh, you don't know a sister," Rochelle said with a smile.

I then smiled and said, "How could I ever forget you?" and gave her a hug. I thought Rochelle was never gonna let me go. Luckily Pam had Nikki on the other side of the yard. It would have been easy to mistake this situation for something else. Rochelle had had a crush on me since high school. Rochelle was very beautiful, but I was never attracted to her—plus she smoked, and I can't stand smoke. I lied to her and told her I thought Pam was looking for her. Rochelle told me she would talk to me later and went looking for Pam. I turned back to Chuck, and he burst out in laughter and said that was quick thinking. I told Chuck Nikki was with Pam and I would introduce him as soon as I got a chance.

Chuck and I mingled and talked to so many people I was wearing down. When Pam and Chuck have a party, they do it big. Besides inviting all the people there, they had hired Morning Mike E, the DJ from Memphis's Hot 97 morning show, to keep the party crunk. I looked and saw Pam and Nikki standing with a group of women. As I was about to make my way over, I heard "What up, Rome?" I turned around, and it was my boy Tank. We greeted each other, and we started walking toward the group of women. As we got closer, Tank said, "Damn! Who is that with Pam?" His eyes were wider than a kid's at Christmas.

I thought I'd have some fun. I said, "I don't know." I knew he was talking about Nikki because Tank knew all the other women in the group.

Damn, I wanted to bust out laughing, but I smiled and bit on my lip when he said "Sit back, son, and watch a player at work." As we approached the ladies, I slowed down and let Tank lead, and I followed. "Hello, ladies," Tank said. They all said hello except for Pam. She knew his ass was up to something. Pam looked at me, and I winked my eye as if to say "Watch this." Tank reached for Nikki's hand, got it, and kissed it. With Tank not noticing, Nikki looked over at me. I smiled, and by me not saying anything, Nikki realized it was Tank, God's gift to women. Nikki smiled, and then she decided to have some fun. Still holding Nikki's hand, Tank said, "Heaven must really be sad right now because they lost an angel."

The group of ladies laughed. Tank took out a pen and wrote his number down on a dollar and gave it to Nikki. Nikki then said, "I knew I felt something when I was a church today when I prayed for God to send me a man." Tank smiled ear to ear, turned, looked at me, and winked, as Nikki paused and then said "Sorry, but it is not you." The group burst out into hysterical laughter. Nikki then told Tank, "I will keep this in case I can't find Romeo. Maybe you might know where he is."

Tank turned and looked at me with his mouth wide open and embarrassed, looking like he could crawl into the first hole he saw. While the group was still laughing, Tank was still looking at me and hesitantly asked, "Nikki?" I shook my head yes with a big smile on my face. Tank looked back at the ladies and said, "I knew it the whole time—I just wanted to trip y'all out." At this point the ladies all had tears in their eyes from laughing. Pam told Tank that was what his none-macking ass got as she wiped her eyes, still laughing. I then officially introduced Tank to Nikki. She then gave him a brotherly hug, and Tank told Nikki, "That was a good one; y'all got me. Gimme my dollar back."

The group burst out with laughter again. "Naw, bro, this is my dollar now." Tank vowed he was gonna get all of us back.

Everybody then sang "Happy Birthday" to Pam, with Chuck leading the way over the loudspeakers. Everybody then formed a line and got some food. Nikki, Tank, Pam, Chuck, and I all sat at one of the picnic tables together. After eating I danced with Nikki. She taught me how to do the Chicago Step, and we had fun as everybody did the Electric Slide. Later, as the party wound down, we were getting ready to leave. I kissed Pam bye and told Chuck I would holler at him later. I told Tank I'd see him at the office tomorrow. Tank looked at me and Nikki, smiled, shook his head, and said, "Man, y'all got me good."

Pam gave Nikki her number and said, "I won't forget we're going shopping one day this week."

Nikki said, "Ok," and she gave Pam a hug, and we left. When I pulled out of Pam's driveway, I asked Nikki if she was ready to go home. She said no. I was a little bit surprised by her answer. I said to myself, Should I ask Nikki if she wants to get in my Jacuzzi? What the hell, I said to myself, and I asked. Nikki said she would love to!

CHAPTER 4

We made it to my house and went in. Nikki then said, Wait, I don't have a bathing suit to put on. I told her I had plenty of T-shirts and shorts that were brand new that she could put on. Nikki said ok. Nikki looked around and said, "My God, this is beautiful."

I looked around and smiled at Nikki and asked her, "What?"

Nikki said, "Your home."

"Oh, thanks," I replied. I went to prepare the Jacuzzi. I told Nikki to make herself at home. I then went upstairs got her clothes and a towel and brought them to her. I told her she could change in the downstairs bedroom. I knocked on the door and asked Nikki if she wanted a drink. She asked what I had. I told her, and we settled on apple martinis. I told her I would be in the Jacuzzi. I went over to the bar and grabbed two glasses and the bottled apple martini out of the fridge. I placed them down by the Jacuzzi and walked over, got my remote, and let the TV screen down. I put the TV on BET—*Midnight Love* was on. I went back over, filled our glasses, got in the Jacuzzi, and waited on Nikki. I turned the TV volume up a little as Prince's "Betcha by Golly Wow!" video played on the screen. The surround-sound speakers kept the music mellow.

Nikki came out of the bedroom and stood shocked and said "Damn! That's sharp" as she watched the screen. Nikki walked toward the Jacuzzi still looking at the screen. I looked at her and said to myself, Damn, she's gorgeous. I got up reached for Nikki's hand and helped her down into the Jacuzzi. We sat down, I handed Nikki her glass, and I got mine. We talked, laughed, sipped on our drinks, and generally had a great time.

"Rome, your home looks like a palace," Nikki said. "I would have never guessed it was this beautiful." I told Nikki thanks again. We talked about everything and really got a kick out of Tank earlier. I told Nikki I was happy she'd had fun and glad she and Pam vibed. I didn't know if it was from the alcohol or sheer nerves, but I asked Nikki if I could kiss her, and before I could get the final word out, Nikki covered my mouth with hers. We kissed passionately for a while. It was getting late; I asked Nikki if she minded spending the night and said I could take her home early enough for her to get dressed and make it to work. Nikki raised an eyebrow and smiled. She said that was fine.

"But," Nikki said, and before she could finish, I said, "No, no, no, you could sleep down here in the guest bedroom."

"That's not what I was gonna say," she said and chuckled.

Nikki told me that what she had been about to say was that she was gonna need another T-shirt and shorts. I laughed and said, "Sure, no problem." Still feeling like an ass, I went upstairs and got them for her. I told Nikki there were extra towels in the bathroom closet when she got ready to shower. After telling Nikki that, I cleaned up our mess around the Jacuzzi before I went upstairs to take my shower. Nikki and I had a long kiss. I then told her good night and went upstairs. I took my shower and got in my bed.

For some reason I found it real hard to sleep tonight. Well, the reason was really knowing that the woman that I had fantasized about was in my house.

I thought about earlier when Nikki got in the Jacuzzi and the shirt she had on got wet and her nipples hardened. I was glad the bubbles covered me because my dick got hard enough to bust through concrete. Then when I was getting the empty bottle and glasses, Nikki got out of the Jacuzzi, and my slightly too-big shorts she was wearing, which were even heavier from the water, fell down around her ankles. I pretended not to see, as I could feel Nikki look around at me. I pretended to have my head down, picking up a glass. But I had seen that beautiful round ass of hers. Nikki was so fine she should have had that body on display in a museum somewhere. I finally got sleepy and dozed off—I knew I had to get up extra early.

I woke up a lot earlier than I thought; really, I don't think I went to sleep. I got up, washed up, got dressed, and went downstairs. I was about to knock on the bedroom door to wake Nikki, but I heard water running in the bathroom, so I knew she was awake. I then went in the kitchen, fixed us breakfast, and poured some orange juice. Nikki came out of the bedroom and into the kitchen. She was fully dressed. Nikki smiled, and looking at the amazement in her eyes, I could tell she was very impressed by my cooking skills. Nikki then said, "Good morning."

I said "Good morning" in return. "How did you sleep?" I asked.

Nikki answered "Like a baby" and smiled.

"That's good to hear. Glad you were comfortable," I said. "Join me," I asked Nikki. We sat down and ate breakfast before we headed out. I dropped Nikki off at her house, she gave me a kiss, and I drove to work. I worked on my client's files the entire morning. After a while it was kind of hard to concentrate when I kept thinking of the weekend I'd just had with Nikki.

I was awakened from my daze when I heard "What's up, Lucky?" It was Tank coming into my office. I asked Tank what was up with him. "Nothing much," he replied. "You still recuperating from the weekend?" Tank asked. Yeah, it was Monday and it felt like it. I was ready for the workday to end. So I concentrated hard and finished the day out. Before I left the office, Nikki called and asked if I could come by her place before I went home and if I could bring my appetite. I smiled and told her ok. I told Tank I was gonna go ahead and leave and that I'd talk with him later.

I went by Nikki's; she opened the door and without hesitation gave me a big wet kiss. Surprised, I asked, "What did I do deserve that?" I smiled.

"Just being you," Nikki said. Nikki had candles lit, and the fragrance from them combined with the Vera Wang perfume she was wearing really aroused me. Nikki had cooked me dinner. She walked me over to the table, sat me down, and told me to wait a minute and she'd be right back. Nikki went in her bedroom, and when she came out, she was wearing a black see-through teddy with black matching thongs and a pair of sexy stiletto heels and no bra. I thought I was going to pass out. I must have looked stupid as hell, because my mouth was flung open and my eyes almost popped out of my head. I said to myself, I've done something right. Without saying a word, Nikki came over to me, loosened my tie, and started to feed me. Nikki fed me steak, mashed potatoes, and green beans. The food was delicious. I willingly ate, but my mind wasn't on food. Nikki must have sensed it too, because in one motion she put the fork down, reached down between my legs, grabbed my dick, and kissed me like she was trying to suck the life out of me. Nikki then stood up, took me by the hand, and led me to her bathroom.

Nikki started undressing me. After she finished, she stroked back and forth on my extremely hard dick as she said, "Oh my God." I didn't know if it was from how hard I was or how big. Nikki stopped stroking me and pulled back her shower curtains. She had run me some hot bathwater with a lot of bubbles. As I got in, Nikki left; she returned with a glass of wine. Nikki took a sip, leaned down and kissed me. Nikki then handed me the glass and told me to lie back in the tub and enjoy. Nikki then proceeded to wash me like I was a king and she was my royal servant. From head to toe, Nikki washed me, and she didn't miss a spot. When she finished, I got out, Nikki dried me off stopping only momentarily to tongue wrestle with me. Nikki then took me by the hand and led me to her bedroom. She then asked me if I was ready for dessert? At this point my mind was still spinning from when I'd first arrived. Still not believing this was actually really happening, I let out a weak yes.

Nikki led me to her bed and told me to lie down. She reached over and picked up a bowl of fruit that she had placed in the room. It was filled with grapes, bananas, peaches, and cherries. Nikki picked up some grapes, held them over my face, and fed them to me. Nikki told me to lie there and not move. I did as she commanded. Nikki then took a banana, slowly peeled it, and licked it very slowly from the tip to the base and back to the tip again. I was gone. Nikki had sent my mind to space and back. Nikki then placed the banana in her mouth and down her throat because over half the banana disappeared in her mouth. Nikki let it stay that way while she took off her teddy and thongs. Now I was really looking at God's gift. Nikki removed the banana and put it to my mouth for me to bite it. She then put it down, picked up a peach, and then straddled me by sitting on my stomach. Nikki leaned over me, bit the peach, held it in her teeth, and came face to face with me. With that type of motion, I knew she wanted me to do the same. So I bit into the peach and held it with my teeth. Both of us were sharing a peach with no hands. Once I had clinched the peach with my teeth, Nikki bit her side. The juice ran down my lips, chin, neck, and body. Nikki then licked every bit of juice that had flowed from the peach down to the center of my body. Nikki then gently bit both my nipples and retraced her licking pattern back down my body. Nikki then gently started sucking and licking the head of my dick. I grabbed her pillow and began to squeeze the life out of it. Nikki then lured her mouth over my shaft and tried to take in the whole thing. But I was too large for her to totally swallow it. But that didn't stop her from trying. I moaned and panted as Nikki was in full control. As Nikki pleased me with her mouth and tongue, I thought back to the time I was in the shower, when I imagined how Nikki felt and masturbated. Then I thought back to the dreams and fantasies of making love to Nikki. But this was no fantasy—it was real, and right now I was living for the moment.

I raised up, kissed Nikki, and positioned her where she was now lying on the bed. I then kissed Nikki from head to toe ever so slowly. I then reached inside the fruit bowl and took out a cherry and popped it in my mouth and proceeded to place my face at Nikki's dripping mound. I then began to masterfully lick and suck Nikki's pearl and pussy lips. Nikki had her nails in my shoulders as my mouth covered her entire twat. Nikki bucked wildly as I gave her a tongue-lashing to remember. I could feel Nikki's body tensing. I knew it wasn't gonna be long before she came. Nikki's moans were loud, and her breathing was heavy.

There was no way she could take much more without coming, so I pushed the cherry out of my mouth past Nikki's pussy lips and into her. I then licked and sucked her clit and lips ravishingly. Nikki grabbed my head with both her hands. When Nikki was at her peak I removed my tongue and placed my lips against her lower lips and sucked in. Nikki screamed as she came violently. The force pushed the cherry back into my mouth along with her sweet juices. I didn't miss a drop as I cleaned her with my tongue, chewed the cherry, and swallowed it. Nikki lay there for a second barely conscious, trying to catch her breath with her eyes closed. When she opened them, I raised up. She smiled, as my face was glazed from her juices. Nikki finally spoke, very hoarse. She said, Damn, boy." I lay on the bed, and Nikki climbed on top of me and rode my dick good and slow. Nikki moaned with each thrust of her hips. She speeded up and rode my dick hard and fast. Nikki's body savored every inch as she cried out from her orgasm.

Then came the grand finale as Nikki positioned herself on her hands and knees. I got behind her and mounted her slow and deep. Nikki was dripping wet at this point from my penetration. I loved the way Nikki felt just as much as she did me. I pumped Nikki with force as her ass bounced back and forth. I could feel Nikki's walls tighten around my dick. I couldn't take much more. That's when Nikki told me she masturbated every night thinking about my dick. That was it—we both came. I came so hard I fell off the bed. Nikki screamed again as she came. Shortly after, her scream turned to laughter after I hit the floor. I had to lie on the floor for a little while from being so weak. I laughed with Nikki. I was so drained I almost fell asleep on the floor. I picked my tired self up and lay back in the bed with Nikki. I didn't know if my heart was still beating fast from the extracurricular activities or because Nikki lay on me the same way she had in my dream when she told me she loved me and I said the same. With my eyes closed, scared to death, I slowly opened one eye and looked down at Nikki. Nikki was sound asleep on my chest. Whew, what a relief. I soon drifted off too.

CHAPTER 5

When we woke up, the sun was shining bright. I looked at the time, and we both were late for work. We looked at each other and laughed. Both of us called in. After that, Nikki and I made love again. Before we knew it, it was one o'clock in the afternoon. As I prepared to leave, we stood at Nikki's front door and kissed. I then patted Nikki on her ass and told her I would see her later. Nikki smiled and said "Bye, baby" and stole one more kiss. I told her bye and I left.

When I made it home, I took a shower, got dressed, and listened to my messages. Both Pam and Tank had left messages. Pam's message was for me to call her back. Tank's message was to tell me he wasn't busy at work today, so he'd handled my clients for me and he'd holler at me later. Good looking out, I thought.

I then called Pam. She told me she was calling to tell me thanks for the bracelet that I gave her on her birthday. I told her she was welcome. Pam then told me how much she'd enjoyed Nikki and said she seemed to be a sweet person. Pam just didn't know how sweet, I thought as a smile crept across my face. "Nikki told me you two are to go shopping this week," I said.

"Yep, we sure are," Pam said.

"Don't teach Nikki any bad habits, big sis."

"Now you know I don't have any bad habits in me, li'l bro."

"Just joking, Pam. I'll talk to you later. Tell Chuck I said what's up."

"Ok, Rome, be good."

Since Nikki had surprised me by cooking me dinner, I wanted to surprise her, so I went by her job. I had gotten Nikki a bouquet of roses, but she wouldn't be in for another twenty minutes, her captain told me. So I left the roses at the station for Nikki. I had attached a card to the roses that asked Nikki if she could meet me on Riverside at the park. When Nikki made it in, her captain handed her the roses. Nikki was surprised and asked, "Who left these for me?"

Her captain (who was female, by the way) said, "One of the most handsome men I ever saw."

Nikki smiled and read the card. She then quickly got her things stored away in her locker, grabbed her keys, and went out the door. Before Nikki could head in the direction of her car, she looked and saw a well-dressed older gentlemen holding a large card with the words "Nikki Adams" on it. And he was standing by an all-white Cadillac stretch limo. Nikki laughed and walked over to the man, who tilted his hat and said, "This way, Ms. Adams," as he opened the door for her. Nikki couldn't stop smiling as the chauffeur drove her to the park. The car stopped, and the man once again opened her door, this time to let her out. When Nikki stepped out, she looked over and saw me. I waved, and Nikki walked over. The man then drove away.

When Nikki made it over to me, she let out a playful scream as she saw I had planned us a picnic. Nikki walked up to me and gave me a kiss. We then sat down on the blanket. I had chicken, corn, rolls, baked beans, wine, and Nikki's favorite dessert: pecan pie. We sat and ate; we fed each other and drank our wine. After eating, we lay on the blanket and talked while we looked at the river. The sun was about to set and the reflection off the water was beautiful. I had driven to the park, so we packed everything up and put it in my truck. I then drove Nikki to her car and told her I would call her when I made it home. I had to run by Tank's house to pick up some files. Nikki said ok. We kissed, and she got in her car, rolled her windows down, and waved at me and then drove off. Damn, I forgot that her air wasn't working in her car.

I started my truck and went by Tank's. When I arrived at Tank's house, he had seen my headlights. He opened the door and went back into his study. I came in, closed the door, and walked down a couple of steps into his study. Tank was like, "What's going on, chief?"

I said, "Nothing much." I then handed Tank a bottle of Moët.

He said, "Shit, I need to do stuff for you more often" and laughed. I then thanked Tank for taking care of my clients for me. Tank said, "Man, it was no big deal, no problem at all. That's how our firm became so successful—we take care of each other and our clients."

"Word," I said. I then got my files, and Tank set his Moët down, gave me a hug, and said thanks. I felt tired and went home.

When I got there, I called Nikki to see if she had arrived home safely. Nikki and I talked for about two hours; she wanted me to meet her mother. At first I felt uneasy, but I quickly told Nikki I would love to. I thought, We are friends with no strings attached, so what could go wrong? Nikki thanked me again for a wonderful evening. Before we hung up, I told Nikki that I would be free on Sunday and we could go by her mother's then. "That's fine," Nikki said. I then told Nikki I had one more special surprise for her, but she would have to wait until Saturday when we went to visit her mother. I could feel and hear the excitement in Nikki's voice as she said, "I got another surprise coming?"

"Yes, you do, but you'll have to wait until Sunday."

"Ok, I'll try," Nikki said as she laughed.

"Ok, we'll talk later," I said.

"Good night," Nikki said.

I replied "You too" and hung up.

The next couple of days, Nikki's mind went haywire, trying to figure out what my surprise was. Was I gonna take her on another picnic? Or was I gonna tell her I loved her? She thought, Or maybe I frightened him when I told him I wanted him to meet my mother. Whatever it is, I have to wait until Saturday to find out. On Saturday Nikki had completed her jogging, finished doing laundry, and cleaned her house. Nikki was trying to do everything in the world to keep from thinking about what I was going to say or do. Nikki was so overcome by anxiety her hands started to sweat.

During the week, I had finished working with my clients and was getting ready to go on a well-deserved two week vacation, since Tank and I had just hired eight new lawyers for our firm. That brought our firm to thirty, which made us a real powerhouse in the industry. So Tank and I really didn't have to work as hard, but since teenagers we had loved working on cases. When we won, it was like an adrenaline rush, and when we lost, it was a very low feeling. So to us the field of law became more of a passion than a job. And now I was taking a short break from Daniels and Miller. When I got up, I worked out, washed my truck, cut my yard, and ran some errands. When I got back I called Nikki. We talked, and I asked her what time she wanted me to come by. Nikki told me around two o'clock would be fine. I told Nikki ok, I would see her at two.

After that I called Pam. Chuck answered and told me Pam wasn't there, that she had gone to the grocery store. I laughed and said, "I should have guessed, since it's Saturday. Anyway, I was calling to see if you guys wanted to go to the Grizzlies game tonight. Tank is going to Miami this weekend, and I got two extra tickets."

"Man, we would be thrilled to go. You know how much your sister loves the Grizzlies," Chuck said. He then asked, "Who are they playing, anyway?" I told him the Lakers. "Shit yeah," Chuck said, "We'll come over to your house around eight."

"Ok, cool," I said. "I'll holler at you then."

I went upstairs, got dressed, and went to Nikki's house. Nikki opened the door looking beautiful as ever. She gave me a kiss and said, "Rome, you are too much." I smiled, as Nikki was referring to the roses I had in my hand for her. I told Nikki I had something in the truck for her mother also. Nikki squeezed me again and gave me another kiss. This time we started to get heated, so we stopped and laughed. I asked Nikki if she was ready, and she said yeah. Nikki set her alarm, and we hurried out and headed over to her mother's house. I asked Nikki on the way if she was ready for her surprise. Nikki sat back, closed her eyes for a second, took a deep breath, exhaled, and said yes. I then pulled out the Memphis Grizzlies tickets and smiled.

Nikki was shocked and relieved at the same time. For three days Nikki hadn't known whether to accept or reject the surprise I had for her. Nikki was relieved to know it wasn't something major, because she didn't know if it was going to be good or bad. Nikki felt a little disappointed—she wasn't the type to expect things from anyone. But Nikki had thought it would be better than basketball tickets. Nonetheless, Nikki leaned over and kissed me on the jaw. I then told Nikki that Chuck and Pam were going with us. Nikki clapped her hands in excitement. I then asked Nikki, "Are you surprised?"

"Very," Nikki said.

"Good," I replied. "I hope the Grizzles win—that would make it even more special."

Nikki was starting to give me directions to her mother's house. Nikki's mother lived in Olive Branch, Mississippi—that's located on the outskirts of Memphis.

CHAPTER 6

We pulled up to a beautiful brick house with a fence and a magnificent garden about twenty yards away. The scenery was captivating. I could see that her mother had a barn and a stable with a couple of horses. It was very quiet and peaceful there. And the air was crisp, clean, and refreshing. There was a rumor I once heard that the people in Mississippi lived longer than anybody else in the world because of its naturalness, and I started to believe that it was more of a fact than a rumor in the short time I was there.

We walked up to the door, and Nikki's mother opened it. She smiled as she said "Hey, my baby" as she hugged and kissed Nikki.

Nikki then said, "Mama, this is Romeo Daniels." I reached out to shake her hand, and she said, "Boy, if you don't give me a hug…" We all laughed as Mrs. Adams hugged me.

Nikki then told me, "This is my angel," speaking of her mother, Mrs. Jean Adams. I could see where Nikki got her beauty from. Nikki's mother was an older version of her, except Mrs. Adams's eyes were a lighter green, and she had a beautiful long black-and-gray highlighted ponytail. Nikki stood there the whole time smiling, looking like she wanted to laugh.

Mrs. Adams said, "Son, I hope you're hungry, because I cooked dinner for us."

"Yes ma'am," I said. That explained the wonderful smell coming from the kitchen and spreading throughout the house. Nikki had given her mom a heads-up earlier in the week that we were coming to visit.

We went into the living room. Nikki and I sat down. Mrs. Adams told us she was almost finished cooking and we would be eating soon. Nikki then got up, followed Mrs. Adams into the kitchen, and asked, "You need me to help you, Mama?"

"No, baby, you just go sit down and entertain our guest."

"Yes ma'am," Nikki said as she kissed and hugged her mother. Nikki came and sat down beside me and took out an old photo album. As we looked at the pictures of Nikki's family, she was explaining who everybody was in the pictures. Nikki showed me photos of Mrs. Adams when she was young. I had Nikki crying with laughter as I said, "Bet your mama was hell in her heyday." Then we came across a picture that made me laugh so loud Mrs. Adams came into the living room and asked if everything was all right.

"Yes, Mama, we're just looking at the photo album," Nikki said.

"Oh," Mrs. Adams said. "Well, dinner is about to start in a matter of minutes," and she disappeared back into the kitchen.

I then looked back at the picture, at Nikki, at the picture again, then at Nikki again. I was laughing the whole time, trying to catch my breath. With tears in my eyes, I told Nikki, "Damn, you were ugly." Nikki burst out laughing. The picture we were looking at was of Nikki when she was ten. Her two front teeth were missing, she had on some big-ass glasses, and her head was nappy as fuck! The only way you could tell it was Nikki was by her dark green eyes. I told Nikki to thank God adulthood had been very kind to her.

Nikki, still laughing, told me, "All right, Rome, enough jonening."

Then Mrs. Adams walked in and told us we could go wash our hands because dinner was ready. Before I washed my hands, I thought, Oh shit, and ran out to my truck. I had forgotten to give Mrs. Adams her roses. I brought them in, and Mrs. Adams was very surprised. She thought they were for Nikki. Nikki told her, "No, Ma, Romeo bought those for you. I got mines earlier." I gave Mrs. Adams the roses, and she gave me a hug. I then went into the restroom and washed my hands.

We all then went into the kitchen. Mrs. Adams had cooked one of my favorite foods, catfish. Mrs. Adams had cooked enough food to feed ten people. I pulled Mrs. Adams's chair out and then Nikki's. "A gentleman as well as handsome," Mrs. Adams said. I smiled and looked at Nikki. Mrs. Adams led us in saying grace, and then we ate. After eating, Nikki told Mrs. Adams to sit down and relax. We cleaned the kitchen, after which it was time to go. The game started at nine, and it was now six o'clock, I hugged Mrs. Adams, told her it was my pleasure to meet her, and said thanks for the great dinner. Mrs. Adams told me I was more than welcome, and she thanked me for the roses. She and Nikki then hugged and kissed. Nikki told Mrs. Adams she would see her later. I opened the truck door for Nikki, walked around to the driver's side, and got in. We waved bye to Mrs. Adams and then left. On the way home, I told Nikki that I could see the beauty resemblance in her and her mother. Nikki said thank you. I then told Nikki, "But for damn sure, you got your daddy's hair." Nikki laughed so hard she couldn't stop coughing. I had to ask her if she was ok. We had a lot of fun.

After a while Nikki noticed I was almost at her house. When I had gone outside to get Mrs. Adams's roses, I'd called Pam and told her to use her key when they made it to my house. I knew I was gonna be a little late. I told Nikki I needed to go by her house because I had to use the bathroom real bad. When we made it, there was a car parked in Nikki's driveway. "Were you expecting anybody?" I asked Nikki. Nikki looked puzzled and said no. I parked on the street because Nikki's car was parked in her garage and the door was down. And this other car didn't leave any room to park behind it in the driveway. We both got out and walked toward the other car to see if we could see someone. Nikki walked in front of me. As we got closer, we could see that there was a red bow on the car. Nikki turned around to face me; I was holding the keys to a brand-new Mercedes-Benz S500 up in the air. I smiled and said, "I hope you like it."

Nikki said "No, no, no, no" as she shook her head in disbelief.

I told Nikki, "I was playing about the tickets earlier. This is your real surprise."

Nikki was like, "Rome, you know I can't accept this."

I told Nikki, "Hey, that's what friends are for. I know that your air is out in your car, and this is the hottest month in the year. Besides, it was no problem getting it for you. The one thing that my parents instilled in me was that if I could help someone—do it. So now do you see? It's not only that I wanted to get it for you but also that I made my parents a promise that I would do something for someone if I could."

Nikki stood there with tears in her eyes and said, "Romeo, please, I can't take…" I cut Nikki off, placed the keys in her hand, and hugged her. Nikki then cried as I stood there holding her.

CHAPTER 7

A year had passed since that day. Nikki and I had been out on numerous dates, but to me it was friendship nothing else. I only hoped that with Nikki it was the same. We never officially said we were a couple. As much fun and as many great times as I'd had with Nikki, I could not give her my heart. I was so caught up in having a good time with her that I didn't consider Nikki's feelings. I was so concerned about getting hurt again, but what about the pain Nikki was gonna feel? I didn't realize Nikki was really into me. So now, without breaking Nikki's heart, I had to ease away from her. And I knew it was not going to be easy.

As the weeks went by, I did everything in my power to pull away from Nikki. The more I avoided Nikki, the more I felt a void. I started working at the firm nonstop. I tried hanging out with Tank, and it still felt like something was missing. I was miserable. I told myself time after time and day after day, I'm ok, and everything is going to be all right. My heart was where I wanted it, with me and nobody else. Nikki must have started to get the hint, because when we talked, it wasn't the same. The fun had ceased and the laughter had stopped. We had even started to argue at times. I began to wonder about our friendship. Everything had changed.

I stopped by Pam's and grabbed me a bite to eat. Pam didn't know it, but I saw her out of the corner of my eye, as she would stare at me when she thought I wasn't noticing. Chuck was in Dallas—his job had a big two-week convention that he had to attend. Pam was missing Chuck like crazy. She tried to keep busy and pass the days away until Chuck came home. When I finished eating, I washed my plate. I looked over, and Pam was staring out the window in the kitchen. I asked, "Are you ok? Pam, what's wrong?" Pam turned toward me with tears streaming down her face. I walked over to her and embraced my sister and told her Chuck would be back soon. At least she missed Chuck and could cry her eyes out, I missed Nikki so much, but I could only cry out of my heart. I knew

Nikki and Pam talked every day on the phone. It took everything in me not to ask Pam about Nikki. I later went home and lay down. Tired as I was, I hadn't slept well in over a month. My appearance had begun to change. I had lost twelve pounds without trying, and I could have used a shave.

I was lying on my sofa one evening when I got a call. It was Pam, and she was furious. "What in the hell is wrong with you?" she screamed.

"What do you mean?" I asked.

"You know what I mean. What in the fuck did you do to Nikki?"

"Pam, Pam, calm down," I said. "What are you talking about?"

"Nikki just left my house with her eyes swollen from crying, and she's not eating or sleeping. You could have told me you had quit her the other day. I watched you, and you have changed, Romeo. Nikki has become my second-best friend for over a year and a half, and I don't want to see her hurt like this. Tell me, little brother, what did she do so bad that you had to treat Nikki like that? Better yet, don't answer my fucking question! I never thought I would see the day that you would turn out to be such a selfish bastard." After saying all that, Pam slammed the phone down and hung up in my face. Pam never gave me a chance to tell her that Nikki and I were just friends. I am a grown-ass man, I thought. How is Pam gonna go off on me? I didn't want Nikki, and if Pam was that upset, why didn't she have a fucking relationship with her? I was so pissed off at this point.

I picked up the phone, getting ready to dial Pam's number back and let her have it. But something stopped me. No matter how Pam's words cut me, I couldn't call back. Because what Pam said was all true. The tune I'd been singing every day since I met Nikki was that my heart belonged to me and no one could have it again. I thought what I'd been telling myself all this time was *bullshit*. Had I really let Keisha take me to this point of never loving again? Why was I acting like some scared little boy? I thought my feelings, mindset, and overall affections had changed. Deep down I knew they had changed. Could it have been that what I once felt for Nikki, lust, had been replaced by love? Whether I wanted to admit it or not, I was in *love* again. No matter how I tried to shake it or ignore it, love had me, and I knew it. Actually, I had known it long ago, when I first met Nikki. I had been afraid and tried to run, but it goes to show no matter how long or how far you run, love catches up with you.

At that moment my phone rang again. Half hesitant to answer it, I said, "Hello."

"Hey, what's up, man?" It was Tank, to my relief. I took a deep breath and said nothing much, then asked what was up with him. "Man, I can't call it," Tank said. Tank then said, "I was calling to ask you—what's going on with you and Nikki?"

Confused, I asked Tank, "What you mean?"

Tank said, "Rome, I just left Pam's house. I was helping Chuck put in a new washer and dryer when Nikki came by. Dude, she was messed up. Look, Rome, I'm not trying to get in your business, but man, Nikki is a good girl that loves you."

"Tank, look here…"

"Wait, Rome. Before you shut me out, just listen to me for a second. Please, Rome, I do a lot of fucked-up shit with women, and I deserve to get dogged out, but you, man, you deserve a girl like Nikki. Rome, she loves you, dog, and I know you love her because the shit is all in your eyes when you talk about her. You two deserve each other, Rome. You are my right-hand man, and I love you. Man, I just want you to wake up before it's too late. With that said, I'm gonna holla at you later," and Tank hung up. Now you know my head was really fucked up. Tank had never come to me on the real like that before. It wasn't what Pam and Tank said to make me admit to myself I was in love with Nikki. It was more that I never thought Pam would come at me like a hurricane. And I never would have ever thought Tank would come to me period.

The next day Pam called me. In her voice I could tell she was still fuming from last night. She called to apologize to me and told me she loved me. Pam then told me something that rocked my world. She said Nikki's mother had a sister in New York that was very sick and Mrs. Adams had been up there over a month. Nikki had been flying back and forth the last two weekends. Pam said, "I wasn't gonna tell you this, but because I love you, I felt you should know. Rome, Nikki quit her job and is moving to New York." Pam told me to wait, and then she finished telling me the story. "Nikki drove her Mercedes over here and told me to give you the keys, and she took a taxi to the airport. Her flight is leaving in thirty minutes."

My heart was racing like a NASCAR race car. I dropped the phone, ran out of my house, and jumped in my truck and blazed to the airport. I lived fifteen minutes away. I was going so fast that if I got stopped the police would take me straight to jail. I ran through red lights and stop signs trying to reach Nikki. When I made it to the terminal, I stopped my truck outside the terminal entrance in the loading zone and left my keys in it. I didn't care—all I wanted to do was find my queen. I ran frantically through the airport trying to find the gate for New York. Finally I found it and rushed in. It was packed, I searched everywhere trying to find Nikki, and I didn't see her, not until the attendant came over the loudspeaker and said "Boarding for New York."

I searched the crowd again and still didn't see Nikki. I looked over the crowd to the entrance of the plane and saw Nikki walking in the corridor leading to the plane. I yelled as I tried to make my way toward her. Nikki turned and looked, and so did the crowd of people. "Baby, I have loved you from the first day I met you." I didn't care who saw or heard me. I was fighting for something bigger than any case I'd ever had. I was fighting for my lifeline, which was Nikki.

At this time airport security grabbed me. It looked like thousands of people were in the airport, and I lost sight of Nikki. Security took me into their office and checked my ID and asked, "What is the problem, Mr. Daniels?" I explained to them why I was running and yelling in the airport. Since 9/11 you could barely breathe in an airport without getting harassed. The sergeant told me I couldn't be running around the airport in that manner. The things he was saying were irrelevant at that point. I really didn't care or pay attention. All I could do was think about how I had lost Nikki forever. I couldn't blame anybody for this; I hated myself because it was my doing. Out the security window, I could see the plane headed to New York take off. My heart sank. The sergeant told me they had had my truck towed and when they finished with me I could go get it out of short-term parking. They then let me go with a warning and gave me my keys. I apologized for my behavior but not for trying to stop Nikki.

I hadn't felt this bad since my parents died. I walked through the terminal, headed out to get my truck. I stepped out the door, getting ready to go to the hour-term parking lot. I looked up and saw Nikki, but my legs felt like they were in quicksand. I slowly walked to her. When I reached Nikki, I hugged her like I was dying and she was my life-support system. Nikki hugged me back as we both stood there crying. I was still hugging her without breaking our embrace or even looking at Nikki to tell her I loved her and would never let her go again.

CHAPTER 8

I took Nikki to my house. Once we were there, I brought her bags in and placed them down. I then picked the phone that I had dropped earlier up off the floor and placed it on the hook. I then turned to Nikki and held her. I gave her a kiss on her forehead and told her I was truly sorry and asked her to forgive me. Nikki looked up at me, not saying a word, and nodded her head yes. I then swooped Nikki up and carried her upstairs to my bedroom. Nikki clung to my neck as she had her face buried in my chest, still crying. I laid Nikki down on my bed fully clothed. I pulled her shoes off and pulled the covers over her, and then I lay down with her and held her all night.

The next morning Pam called and was really worried and wanted to know what had happened. Nikki was lying on me, still asleep. I asked Pam if she could drive the car over later. Pam said yeah, she'd have Chuck follow her. She then asked again what had happened. I told Pam I promised I would tell her everything when she came over later.

"Well, just tell me, Rome—are you ok?"

I told Pam yeah, I was ok, and I loved her. Pam said, "I love you too." I then told her I'd see her later.

I rubbed Nikki's beautiful face, as her head was still on my chest. She looked so peaceful that I didn't want to wake her. I eased out of bed, still wearing the clothes I'd had on last night. I went in my bathroom, closed the door, and ran Nikki a hot bubble bath. When she woke up, she could get in and relax. I then went downstairs and took a shower. When I got out, I put my clothes on and fixed breakfast for Nikki. I then took it upstairs to her. Nikki was awake, and she wasn't really hungry. But I fed her a small piece of toast and a couple of bites of eggs, and Nikki drank a small amount of juice. I told her that she had a hot bubble bath waiting on her. Nikki said thanks. I told her Pam would be by later. Nikki said ok. Nikki then got up and went into the bathroom; I gave her my extra bathrobe and told her I would bring her bags upstairs so she could figure out what she was going to wear.

Nikki said thanks. I closed the bathroom door and went downstairs, and I brought Nikki's bags up.

I then went back downstairs and fixed me a cup of coffee. I sat down at the kitchen table and tried to figure out when would be the appropriate time to tell Nikki everything. Nikki had barely spoken since our ordeal at the airport yesterday. One thing I was not going to do was rush her, because we were gonna have to go through a healing process. No matter what it took to make things right, I was willing to do it. I couldn't wait for Pam to arrive. She was gonna be so shocked to see Nikki. I hadn't told Pam that Nikki was here, and I hadn't told Nikki that Pam was bringing her car. I just wanted to see Nikki happy again and try to get back to the way we used to be. Nikki walked in the kitchen, and I stood up and asked if she wanted some coffee. Nikki said no thanks, she was fine. Not really knowing what to say, I asked Nikki if she would have dinner with me later, and if it was ok with her, could we talk? Nikki said sure.

At that moment the doorbell rang. I went into the living room and opened the door. It was Pam and Chuck. "Hey," I told them, "thanks for bringing the car." Pam gave me a hug and the keys. Chuck and I greeted in the brotherly way, and they came on in.

Pam was walking to sit down on the couch when Nikki walked out of the kitchen and into the living room. Pam screamed and ran over and hugged Nikki. "What's going on, girl?" Pam asked.

Nikki, smiling, said, "Nothing, girl."

Chuck then went over and hugged Nikki. "How you feeling?" Chuck asked.

"I'm doing fine," Nikki said. Pam looked over at me and knew I couldn't explain what had happened yesterday, at least not in front of Nikki. I looked backed at Pam, smiled, and thought, Nosy ass. I went over to Nikki and kissed her on her cheek.

Pam said, "Awww." Then she said she and Chuck were headed downtown to Jillian's and wanted to know if Nikki and I wanted to go bowling with them. I told Pam thanks but no thanks—we had other plans. "Well," Pam said. She smiled and told Nikki, "I'll talk to you later." Nikki smiled and then hugged Pam bye and waved at Chuck. Pam and Chuck left.

I asked Nikki, "What you want to do now?"

I was shocked by her answer. Nikki said, "Talk."

I was happy we didn't have to wait until dinner and that Nikki had chosen the time. Man, I was relieved because I didn't want to pressure Nikki into having a discussion she wasn't ready to have. I asked

Nikki to please have a seat on the sofa. I went to the kitchen and got us some bottled water. I didn't know what Nikki was gonna say, but I knew what I had to say. I knew my throat would be dry by the time I finished begging for forgiveness. I walked back in and handed Nikki her water. Then I sat down beside her on the sofa, took a deep breath, and waited on Nikki to begin.

Nikki then said, "Well, you found me at the airport. So I'm going to assume that you know I quit my job and that I'm moving to New York. Romeo, I fell in love with you a long time ago, and I thought at the time you loved me too. As bad as I wanted to be right, I was wrong. After all the things you told me about how Keisha had hurt you and deceived you, I said there's no way in the world that I could do something like that to you. But Romeo, you turn around and do those things to me. I only tried to be good to you and make you happy. But I felt like you led me on, and that hurt me deep because you had my heart. The way you treated me, I felt lower than dirt and then there were times that I really needed you and you wouldn't return my calls. Rome, I wish you would have told me in the beginning your true feelings and I would have known where we stood," Nikki said.

As bad as I wanted to say something, I was determined to hear Nikki out without interrupting. I bit on my lip to keep from talking. Nikki continued, "You are the first guy I ever introduced to my mother. I just thought there was something special about you, Romeo. You took me to the clouds and made me laugh. That was something I was missing for a long time. It wasn't about the material things—I could care less about that. But it was the little things that made me fall for you as deep as I did. Then all of a sudden, Romeo, you brought my world crashing down. The only reason I didn't get on that plane is that I wanted to know why. I'm at least owed that much. And before you start talking, last night you asked me to forgive you. Well, Romeo, I do forgive you, but that's only because I don't want to leave with a burden on my heart. Now tell me what I did wrong," Nikki said.

"Nikki, first of all, I want to start by telling you that with all my heart, I'm very sorry. The last thing in the world I wanted to do was hurt you, Nikki. Baby, I don't want you to ever feel like you did something wrong. It was me being selfish. I was so afraid to let my true feelings show, scared that I would get hurt again. I was blinded to your heart and feelings. Nikki, I want you to know this, baby. Please believe me when

I tell you not one time have I ever thought of you being less than the most beautiful woman I ever met, a woman with a lot of class. I lied to myself over and over again that you and I were just friends. Nikki, the truth is, baby, I have loved you since I laid eyes on you. Baby, every day I spent without you was hell. Inside I was dying. When I tried to pull away, which was only stupidity on my part, I felt my world crumble, Nikki. Baby, you have taught me how to love, really love, and Nikki, I know I love you. Nikki, you are my world and my breath. Without you, baby, I can't breathe. You touched something deep inside me that I can't explain. Baby, I deeply, deeply want to tell you that I am very sorry and regret everything negative that I have created." With that said, I could feel the tears starting to well up in my eyes. I told Nikki again that I loved her. At this time emotions were so high it was hard to talk.

I then stood up and took Nikki by the hand, and she stood up. I then told her, "Baby, I know you are going to New York, and I know that your aunt is sick. Nikki, baby, I don't want to pressure you, but will you move in with me?" The expression on Nikki's face didn't change. "Nikki, I don't want you to answer me now. I want you to go to New York and clear your head, and baby, please take all the time you need. You can take the seven o'clock flight out tonight, and if you come back to me, I know your flight will arrive back here on Monday at six in the evening, and I will be at the airport waiting for you. And I'll know if you aren't on the flight you made your decision that you aren't coming back to me."

Nikki stood there with tears in her eyes and only said "Ok, we'll see what happens." We then kissed, and I went upstairs, got Nikki's bags, put them in the car, and handed her the keys. Nikki and I hugged and kissed. Nikki then got in her car and backed out of the driveway and drove off as I stood there. I was scared, but this time it was for a whole other reason. I wasn't running from love this time—I was trying to hold on to love. The next two days were really going to test me. The agonizing reality started—I didn't know if Nikki was coming back to me or if that was my last time holding her. God forbid. I thought back to when I'd told Nikki at the airport that I would never let her go again. I truly meant it. If Nikki didn't come back to me, she would always be in my heart.

The next two days seemed like forever. On Monday I was sitting in the airport terminal waiting anxiously, as I had arrived one hour early. The flight landed, and I went to the arrival gate. People started getting off the plane, finding their loved ones. People laughed, kissed, hugged, and cried. As I watched and waited for Nikki to appear, she never showed. Standing in shock, I saw that the plane doors were closed only after the pilots and stewardesses exited. With my eyes widened and pulse quickened, I asked one of the pilots, "Excuse me—are there any more passengers on the plane?" In my heart I knew the plane was empty.

The pilot told me, "No sir. We were the last ones."

I was sick; I put my head down and walked out of the airport. Once outside I looked around, hoping Nikki was outside waiting. Not this time. Nikki had made her decision to stay in New York. I felt so bad I almost threw up.

CHAPTER 9

When I arrived home, I pulled up in my driveway and just sat for a moment to reflect on the things I had done, and the tears started to roll down my face. I wiped my eyes, got out of my truck, and went in the house and turned on my lights. "Surprise!" everyone shouted as I almost jumped out of my skin. I didn't know what in the hell was going on.

Pam came over to me, hugged me, and said, "We planned this party for you because you needed it, Romeo. We all know your spirits have been down a lot lately." Pam had organized a party for me on the worst night of my life. She had instructed everybody to park in the back—that's why I didn't see any cars when I arrived. Everybody was there: my family, my friends, Tank and some of the guys from the firm. Pam told me she had waited for me to leave the house. Then she'd used her key, come in, and decorated the place. I then told Pam that I was sorry but I didn't feel like having a party. Even with all the people here that I loved, I didn't feel any better. The love that I needed I had lost.

I then asked Pam, "How did you know I was leaving my house, anyway?" Pam smiled nervously, turned, and looked upstairs; Nikki was standing at the top of the steps smiling at me. I ran up the steps, grabbed Nikki, and kissed her. The people downstairs cheered. I walked forward and Nikki walked backward as we held each other. I guided Nikki into my bedroom and closed the door; I could hear the people downstairs laughing. I looked Nikki in those gorgeous green eyes and said, "I love you."

Nikki told me her aunt was doing much better and that she had done as I said: taken her time and cleared her mind. She knew where her heart belonged. Nikki then said she had gotten an earlier flight back to Memphis. "When I arrived, I called Pam to see if you were there. Pam told me no, that you weren't over at her house. When I made it over, we talked, and I told Pam you asked me to move in with you. And I was ready. So Pam told me not to let you know I was back yet, and she planned this party for us." I stood there speechless, just smiling and looking at my angel, not believing this was really happening Nikki told me "I'll finish with you later" as she gave me a kiss. Nikki then said, "Let's not keep our guests waiting." We then did something together that seemed like a lost art between us. We laughed, and then we went back downstairs to cheering and applauding.

Tank came up to me and hugged me. Man, this dude continued to shock me. I laughed when Tank said "Damn, I got a rep to uphold," and when he let me go as if to say "My bad," we laughed. Everybody was coming over to Nikki and me congratulating us and wishing us well. Now it was a party. I was feeling good, and I had my baby back. I felt on top of the world.

Later, when everybody started to leave, I thanked everyone for making my night so special. With my arm around Nikki, I kissed her on her cheek. There were a few people still at the house; they were getting their things so they could leave. So I thought I would make the wisecrack "You don't have to go home, but you got to get the hell outta here." Everybody laughed.

Finally everyone was gone, and it was only me and Nikki. The house was a mess, but I didn't even care.

Nikki walked up to me, locked her arms around my neck and said, "I hope you didn't get too tired from the party, 'cause you still got work to do." With a devilish grin and an eyebrow arched, I once again swept Nikki up off her feet and took her upstairs. We made it to the bedroom. I laid her down on the bed, and this time I took everything off of her. My sheets weren't gonna be Nikki's cover this time—I was. Nikki's body glistened, I licked my lips as I salivated and hungered for her. It had been a while since we had made love. Nikki, lying on the bed smiling, looked at me and asked, "Are you gonna undress and join me?" I think I was butt-ass naked before she got the word "me" out. As I kissed Nikki like never before, I could tell it was very different this time. It was real. I didn't hide my true feelings from Nikki or myself, and from Nikki's moans I sensed she could tell also. I licked Nikki from head to toe, not missing a spot on her body. Nikki's body quivered. I smiled and thought, Like old times.

Then my tongue went to work. I licked and sucked on Nikki's juice-filled lips like there was no tomorrow. Then I smothered that pearl. I took my time eating Nikki like I was a legendary artist at work. Nikki constantly wiggled and bucked as I slammed my face in out of her mound. Nikki then gave me my favorite drink, Nikki a-la-crème, as her juice flooded my face. I raised up on my knees. Nikki then positioned herself on her hands and knees, face to face with my dick—it looked like a square-off between a cobra and a mongoose. Nikki opened her mouth and engulfed my head. Nikki sucked it hard and slow while her tongue circled the head. Nikki drove me crazy as she tried to suck my entire dick into her mouth. This felt so damn good I thought I was gonna pass out while Nikki sucked my dick with authority. I leaned over and slid a finger inside Nikki. Nikki moaned in response to my finger, then raised her ass a little higher in the air, and I inserted a second finger into Nikki. I felt myself about to come, so I pulled out of her mouth and removed my fingers. I didn't want to come yet, so I waited for a little while before I penetrated Nikki. Nikki looked at me and licked her lips; I then looked Nikki in her eyes and licked her sweet cream from my fingers. Nikki then pushed me down on the bed, and she got on top of me. I didn't know if it was me or if Nikki was trying to make up for lost time. You would have sworn she was a professional horse jockey from the way she rode my dick. I moaned and damn near begged Nikki to stop from her feeling so good. If I had been guilty of something, at this point I would have been confessing to Nikki like she was a priest. Nikki threw her head back and screamed as she let go of all the pressure, stress, and built-up tension that was inside her.

Nikki fell limp on top of me, both of us breathing heavy. I turned Nikki on her back and slowly climbed between her legs. I then buried myself inside her soaked opening. I then pumped Nikki slow, soft, and hard all at the same time. This time I made love to her with a purpose. As I felt myself building up to explode, I started whispering in her ear as I nibbled on it. I told Nikki in a low, deep voice that this was her dick and nobody else's and that she could have it whenever she wanted it. Nikki moaned, "Oh, Romeo."

I then told Nikki, "If you want to come on it, baby, don't hold back." This drove Nikki wild as she pumped back at me. I told Nikki this over and over. Nikki gyrated her hips underneath me as I came deep within my queen. At the same time, Nikki screamed again as she came violently from the mental stroking. This time I collapsed on top of Nikki. We lay there with me still deep inside her. Every once in a while I could feel Nikki squeezing me with her vaginal muscles. She milked me dry. We then fell asleep.

When we woke up the next morning, I ran a hot bubble bath for the both of us. We washed and fondled each other, and then we dried each other off. We got dressed, and Nikki drove me to Waffle House for breakfast. We really enjoyed each other. We laughed, kissed, and fed each other—in general we had fun. I told Nikki I loved her and for the last time apologized to her for my actions. Nikki told me as she smiled, but as serious as hell, "If you ever pull some shit like that again, I will fuck you up." I smiled at Nikki and promised her never again, and we sealed it with a kiss.

When Nikki first moved in with me, I asked her if she owned her own business what it would be. Nikki thought for a minute and then said a small beauty shop. So I got her one. Nikki had her own beauty shop in North Memphis called Nikki's Place. Nikki spent a lot of time in her shop. She had four stylists, not including herself. The word spread about Nikki's Place, and she got a great clientele.

One day, when we finished eating breakfast, I dropped Nikki off at her shop and told her I would bring her car back. One of the stylists was gonna do Nikki's hair, and I was headed to the barbershop. We were going to one of Taylor Price's plays the next evening. After I finished at the barbershop, I went to meet Tank at his house. Tank and I were going fishing. I had Tank follow me by Nikki's shop so I could drop her car and keys off. Nikki told me that when she finished getting her hair done, she and Pam were going shopping so she could find a dress for the play. I said ok. I gave her a kiss and told her I loved her and went go in the car with Tank, and we headed to the lake.

We made it to the lake. It was quiet. There were only four people there. We found a nice spot in the shade and started fishing, and we talked while we fished. I told Tank, "Thanks for calling me that night. Man, I owe you big time."

Tank then said, "Look here, Rome—you don't owe me anything. I wanted to thank you for opening my eyes, man. I have changed my outlook on women. Better yet, life. Rome, because of you I sat back and took a long, hard look at myself. I then said to myself, I wouldn't like it if a guy treated my mother or my sister the way I've treated some women. Hell no, I would want to kill that dude. So Rome, because of you, I did some soul searching. By the way, I've been seeing someone," Tank said.

I smiled at Tank and asked, "Who?"

Tank said, "Gina."

I was like, "Who's Gina?"

"Gina Norris," Tank replied with a big smile on his face.

I was like, "Oh shit! You playing with me." Gina was one of the lawyers we had hired to work at the firm.

"No shit," Tank said. "We've been going out for six months now." I then told Tank congratulations, and we locked hands in our brotherly handshake. At that point Tank got a bite on his line. Tank pulled and pulled, and he yelled, "Rome, help me get the big monster!" I was about to help Tank when he pulled his line out of the water. Tank had caught the smallest fish in the world! We cried laughing.

When I made it home, Nikki was sitting on the sofa, talking to her mom on the phone. I walked over and gave Nikki a quick, quiet kiss without interrupting her conversation. I then walked toward the kitchen and yelled, "Hey, Mama."

Nikki laughed and yelled back at me, "Mama said, 'Hi, Romeo.'"

I got my bottled water, walked back in the living room, and asked, "How's my baby?"

Nikki was off the phone. She replied, "I'm fine. I got a nice dress today, but you can't see it until tomorrow," Nikki said as she hugged and kissed me. "Ooh, you stink bug! You smell like fish," Nikki said.

"I know, baby," I said, and I drank my bottled water. I then went upstairs and got in the shower. After

I washed the suds off and out of my eyes, Nikki was standing there watching me shower. I smiled and asked, "You getting in?"

"No, no, baby. I just got my hair done. Boo. But I'll dry you off," Nikki said. I then said, "I bet you will."

After showering I put on my basketball shorts and T-shirt. Then Nikki and I went downstairs to the den, cuddled, and watched a movie. We were lying down on giant pillows that we placed on the floor. Not really paying attention to the movie, I kept planting little kisses on Nikki's neck and earlobes. Shortly after I fell asleep, after the movie ended, Nikki woke me up so we could go upstairs and go to bed.

CHAPTER 10

The next day we had been out all day. Nikki went by her shop; then I went by the firm, and we went by Pam's. Later we came home and started getting dressed to go to the play. I got dressed upstairs, and Nikki got dressed downstairs. She wanted to surprise me with the new dress she had bought. I got dressed in my all-white Versace dress shirt and my black Armani slacks and vest. I could have easily been mistaken for Michael Jordan. When I went downstairs, Nikki came out of the room and said, "Hi, handsome." Then she asked, "You like?" as she did a twirl for me in her dress.

I smiled from ear to ear. All I could say was "Damn, damn, damn," like Florida Evans. Nikki was beyond beautiful—tonight she was radiant. Nikki looked astonishing in her black Prada dress with matching heels. Nikki was a knockout.

I kissed her. She said "Baby, you're gonna mess up my makeup" and laughed.

"I can't help it; you shouldn't have been so beautiful," I said. Then I told Nikki, "Come on, baby, so we won't be late. You know Taylor Price is the only black man that says his show starts at seven, and it starts at seven."

Nikki laughed. We went out, got in the limo, and went to the play. After the play I took Nikki out for dinner at the Peabody Memphis. The waiter took our order, and I ordered red-label Moët for the both of us. Nikki and I sat at the table talking and still laughing about the play we had just left. Nikki told me to excuse her as she went to the ladies' room. The waiter brought out a chilled bottle of red-label Moët and two glasses already filled. He placed them down and left. Nikki returned. I stood up and pulled her chair out for her. I placed Nikki's glass in front of her, and I got mine. I told Nikki I wanted to give her something. I pulled a black velvet box from my pocket. Nikki's eyes widened, and she started breathing heavy as I told her "This is for you" and opened the box. Nikki almost cut her smile completely off as I handed her a pearl necklace. Nikki was very disappointed but tried not to show it. "That's beautiful," she said as she tried to keep up the happy act.

The waiter returned with our food. Thank God, Nikki thought. She then pretended to be happy as I placed the necklace on her.

"I hope you like it," I said.

"I love it," replied Nikki. Nikki thought, I do love the necklace, but I thought Romeo was gonna ask me to marry him when I saw the jewelry box. How could I have been such a fool?

As we ate our dinner and drank our Moët, Nikki seemed quiet. "Anything wrong?" I asked.

"No, I'm just a little tired. That's all," Nikki said.

As Nikki was about to drink some of her Moët, I called the waiter over. "Yes sir," he said.

"I have a problem." Nikki looked at me, puzzled, as she continued to drink. The waiter asked me what was it. "Sir," I said in a forceful manner, "something is in my friend's glass." Nikki, scared, quickly removed the glass from her mouth. With panic Nikki looked in her glass. There was a five-carat diamond ring in her glass of Moët. Nikki looked at me, confused and in disbelief, as I said, "Baby, will you marry me?"

Nikki said, "Romeo, don't. Please don't play with me like that!"

I got up from the table and went down on one knee. As I took the ring from the glass and said, "Nikki, I want you to be my wife," Nikki knew I was serious.

"Yes, Romeo, I'll be your wife," she said as the tears came streaming from her eyes. I placed the ring on her finger, raised up, and kissed the tears from Nikki's eyes. Nikki stood up. We kissed and embraced as Nikki sobbed. The people in the restaurant cheered for us. I was so nervous I thought my legs were gonna give out. But I wouldn't show Nikki I was nervous. We went home that night and made passionate love.

Three weeks had passed since I had asked Nikki to marry me. I couldn't wait for Nikki to become Mrs. Nikki Daniels. Nikki worked closely with the wedding planners to make sure everything was perfect, from the arrangements down to the music. Tank, Chuck, and I all went and got fitted for our tuxedos. Nikki and the girls had already gotten fitted for their dresses. Nikki and I made sure everybody and everything was in place two weeks before the wedding. We were about to take a getaway trip to Las Vegas. We wanted to go have fun, to take a break from everything. Nikki and I wanted to come back worry- and stress-free. Neither Nikki nor I knew that Chuck and Tank had planned my bachelor party and that Pam and Gina had planned Nikki's wedding shower. On Monday we were leaving for Vegas. Pam, Chuck, Tank, and Gina were going with us. Once in Vegas we had a great time. We unwound and went to all the casinos and a lot of the shows. Las Vegas was beautiful. The getaway was great.

We returned home the following week. It felt good to be back home; Nikki called her mother when we made it in. Nikki told Mrs. Adams she had only three days to get to Memphis because the wedding was Saturday. Mrs. Adams told Nikki not to worry—she'd be there. I told Nikki that I was gonna run by the firm for a minute and I would be back. I gave her a kiss, and I left. Nikki continued to talk to Mrs. Adams. It was after eight o'clock, so I tried to hurry to run in and sign the files that I had requested. When I made it, everyone had already left for the evening. I went in my office, and sure enough the files were on my desk like I asked. When I was finishing up, my phone rang. I answered it, and it was Nikki. She asked if I could stop by her shop and get the money out of the safe so she could deposit it in the morning. I told Nikki, "Yeah, I can do that. Then I will be on my way home."

"Ok, baby," Nikki said. It was no problem. I had to pass her shop anyway. I then told Nikki that I was leaving my office now and that I loved her and would see her in a little while. Nikki said she loved me too, and we hung up. I then left, heading to Nikki's shop. It started to rain.

When I made it to Nikki's shop, the rain had become a downpour. I jumped out of my truck, went and unlocked the door, ran in, opened the safe, and got the money. I then came out. As I was locking the door to the shop, I heard someone say, "Give me your wallet." I tried to turn around; everything stopped, and there was a loud blast. At first I thought it was thunder. Then it happened again. This time I saw where it came from, and a flash of fire came with it. As I fell to the ground, I tried to move, but I couldn't. I looked, and two guys were pulling on my clothes and going through my pockets.

All of a sudden I heard, "Freeze!" It was the police. The guys ran, and the officer chased them. I again tried to move, but I couldn't. I looked down, and I could see the rain was washing blood out to the street. I then realized I had been shot. Twice! I lay in the rain motionless, unable to move. I heard sirens coming from all directions.

When I opened my eyes, everything was blurry. I had to focus. When I did, I saw Nikki sitting in a chair next to me, holding my hand and crying.

I looked around the room, and I saw Chuck holding Pam and Tank holding Gina. They all had tears in their eyes. I couldn't talk. I tried, but there were all types of tubes and cords hooked up to me. I had this one tube down my throat. It freaked me out. With my eyes half opened, I looked back at Nikki. Nikki said, "Thank you, God." Everybody looked and came over by the bed. Nikki got up from her seat. Her beautiful eyes were red and puffy from crying, Nikki then said, "Romeo, I love you, baby. I love you."

Pam came over and started rubbing my head. I could hear her say through her now-cracking voice, "Rome, you've got to get well. You got to. I lost Mom and Dad, Rome. I can't lose you too. Please, Rome, if you can hear me, please," Pam pleaded. Tank and Chuck both walked up with tears running down their faces. They rubbed my hand and arm. Tank couldn't take it and walked out. Gina, with tears in her eyes, followed him.

Chuck told me, "Come on, kid, fight—you gotta fight." Chuck then took Pam out of the room. I could hear her starting to get hysterical.

Now it was only me and Nikki. She kissed me on my jaw. I felt her tears fall on my face. Nikki told me, "See, Romeo? Everybody is upset. You got to get better, baby." I was so tired. My eyes would open and close. Nikki then told me the police had caught the guys that did this—they were on drugs. Nikki stood there talking to me in a calm voice while the tears never stopped running down her face. She was a true angel. Nikki then again told me, "Rome, you've got to get better, sweetheart, not only for Pam, Tank, and me but also for our baby. Romeo, I'm pregnant." Tears rolled down my face. I was so happy I wanted to jump up, grab Nikki, and hold her, never letting go.

All of a sudden, the sound in the room changed from calm to panic as my eyes closed and I couldn't open them. I could hear Nikki scream, "Nurse! Nurse!" And I could tell a lot of people rushed into the room. The last thing I saw was Nikki's beautiful face, and the last thing I heard was Nikki screaming "No, no, no," a flatline sound, and "Code red, code red, code red!"

It was cool outside. Everybody was dressed up; the church was packed. I wouldn't have ever guessed in a million years that so many people cared about me. Pam was still wiping her tears. Nikki had to use eye drops as she tried to stop herself from shaking and remain calm. Tank wore his shades to hide his tears until he went inside the church. When the music started, some people started crying, and everybody stood up.

Tears then streamed from my eyes as I watched my beautiful bride walk down the aisle toward me. Our wedding had been pushed back until the fall because I had to heal, but it finally was happening, our day when we became Mr. and Mrs. Romeo Daniels. This goes to show that if you love someone, let that person know—don't hide it. Because you never know who will capture your heart.

Always let your true feelings show and "never say never."

ABOUT THE AUTHOR

Tony L. Smith was born and raised in Memphis, Tennessee and now resides in Southern California. A newcomer to the writing world, Tony has always been captivated by the art of storytelling, especially the twists and turns that define great novels. It was this fascination that inspired him to start writing, fulfilling a lifelong passion to give readers stories that engage, challenge, and inspire.

www.ingramcontent.com/pod-product-compliance
Lightning Source LLC
LaVergne TN
LVHW092055060526
838201LV00047B/1409